Tater Tot

At The Chase

A Happy Helper

Written by Laura Holman Byrne
Illustrated by Evan Quel

Tater Tot at the Chase
A Happy Helper
Laura Holman Byrne
AllonsYee! Publishing

AllonsYee!
PUBLISHING

Published by AllonsYee! Publishing
Copyright ©2018 Laura Holman Byrne
All rights reserved.

This book was inspired by the wonderful people and places in Tater Tot's life. Other than those people who agreed to be directly identified, all characters, businesses, and events are fictitious.

Publisher's Cataloging-In-Publication Data
(Prepared by The Donohue Group, Inc.)

Names: Byrne, Laura Holman, author. | Quel, Evan, illustrator.
Title: Tater Tot at the Chase. A happy helper / written by Laura Holman Byrne ; illustrated by Evan Quel.
Other Titles: Happy helper
Description: Saint Louis, Missouri : AllonsYee! Publishing, [2018] | Interest age level: 004-012. | Summary: "A Happy Helper shows us how a sweet bulldog named Tater Tot is so eager to help others, he puts his friend Chef Paul in a difficult position and almost ruins someone's birthday. Through the kindness and patience of his family and friends, Tater Tot learns how he let others down and even repays Chef Paul's kindness by enlisting all his friends to help save the birthday party!"--Provided by publisher.
Identifiers: ISBN 9781732771703 (hardback) | ISBN 9781732771710 (paperback) | ISBN 9781732771727 (ebook)
Subjects: LCSH: Bulldog--Juvenile fiction. | Birthday parties--Juvenile fiction. | Helping behavior--Juvenile fiction. | CYAC: Bulldog--Fiction. | Birthday parties--Fiction. | Helpfulness--Fiction. | BISAC: JUVENILE FICTION / Animals / Dogs. | JUVENILE FICTION / Animals / Pets. | JUVENILE FICTION / Bedtime & Dreams.
Classification: LCC PZ7.1.B96 Ta 2018 | DDC [E]--dc23

Dedicated to Ann, Paul, family, friends, and everyone learning or teaching life's lessons.

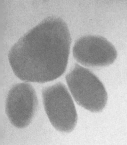

Tater Tot has a smushy face, white fur
with black-and-brown heart-shaped patches,
and a tail curled up like a cinnamon bun!

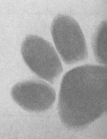

Tater Tot starts each day with a stretch down, a stretch up, some breakfast, and then he's out the door for a new adventure.

Tater Tot waves to MacKenzie, who checks in the guests. Then he says hello to Ms. Kris, the concierge, who knows all the fun places to go!

"Oh, Tater Tot!" cries Rose.
"Please take this menu to Chef Paul.
The birthday party begins very soon!"

Tater Tot's ears jump to the top of his
head as he replies, "Happy to help."

As Tater Tot trots toward the kitchen, Ann,
the engineer, asks, "Tater Tot, will you hold
this new light bulb while I take the broken
light bulb out?" Tater Tot is happy to help.

Sweet Ms. Janet, who lives on the thirty-fourth floor, needs help pushing the elevator button. Jim needs help tying a bow. Kuo needs help finding his pencil.

Tater Tot finally heads to the kitchen, feeling so great about helping everyone!

-MENU-
Appetizer
Soup/Salad
Entree
Dessert
Coffee

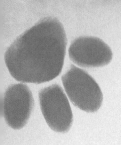

"Tater Tot, what took you so long?
We are almost out of time!" Chef Paul cries.

Tater Tot explains how he just helped everyone.

"You are very kind to help, but you said you
would bring the menu right away. We counted
on you," Chef Paul gently explains. "Now
run along. We have to rush or the birthday
guests will be mad they have no lunch!"

Tater Tot's ears slide down to his chin. He is
sorry he created this problem for Chef Paul and
the birthday guests. As Tater Tot's eyes fill with
tears, he hears the most fantastic singing.

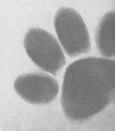

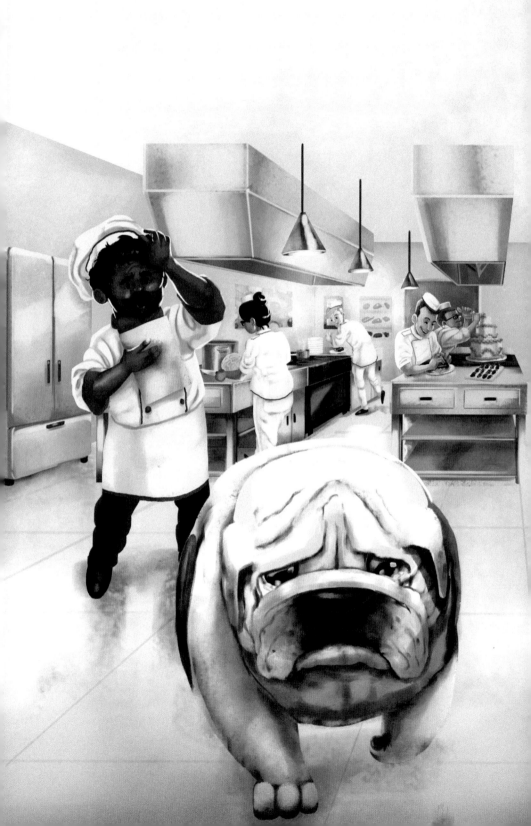

Someone's lively, booming voice
wraps around his ears like a warm hug.
Tater Tot realizes he is smiling,
even though he is still sad.

"Larry!" cries Tater Tot as he sees
the most wonderful bellman in the
world. "What are you singing?"

"My mother's favorite song!" says
Larry. "She taught me so many."

Tater Tot's ears jump from his chin to the top of
his head so fast that fur falls off each side!

"I know exactly how you can
help," Tater Tot tells Larry.

Tater Tot

At The Chase

A Happy Helper

Written by Laura Holman Byrne
Illustrated by Evan Quel

Tater Tot at the Chase
A Happy Helper
Laura Holman Byrne
AllonsYee! Publishing

AllonsYee!
PUBLISHING

Published by AllonsYee! Publishing

This book was inspired by the wonderful people and places in Tater Tot's life. Other than those people who agreed to be directly identified, all characters, businesses, and events are fictitious.

Publisher's Cataloging-In-Publication Data
(Prepared by The Donohue Group, Inc.)

Names: Byrne, Laura Holman, author. | Quel, Evan, illustrator.
Title: Tater Tot at the Chase. A happy helper / written by Laura Holman Byrne ; illustrated by Evan Quel.
Other Titles: Happy helper
Description: Saint Louis, Missouri : AllonsYee! Publishing, [2018] | Interest age level: 004-012. | Summary: "A Happy Helper shows us how a sweet bulldog named Tater Tot is so eager to help others, he puts his friend Chef Paul in a difficult position and almost ruins someone's birthday. Through the kindness and patience of his family and friends, Tater Tot learns how he let others down and even repays Chef Paul's kindness by enlisting all his friends to help save the birthday party!"--Provided by publisher.
Identifiers: ISBN 9781732771703 (hardback) | ISBN 9781732771710 (paperback) | ISBN 9781732771727 (ebook)
Subjects: LCSH: Bulldog--Juvenile fiction. | Birthday parties--Juvenile fiction. | Helping behavior--Juvenile fiction. | CYAC: Bulldog--Fiction. | Birthday parties--Fiction. | Helpfulness--Fiction. | BISAC: JUVENILE FICTION / Animals / Dogs. | JUVENILE FICTION / Animals / Pets. | JUVENILE FICTION / Bedtime & Dreams.
Classification: LCC PZ7.1.B96 Ta 2018 | DDC [E]--dc23

Dedicated to Ann, Paul, family, friends, and everyone learning or teaching life's lessons.

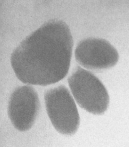

Tater Tot has a smushy face, white fur
with black-and-brown heart-shaped patches,
and a tail curled up like a cinnamon bun!

Tater Tot starts each day with a stretch down, a stretch up, some breakfast, and then he's out the door for a new adventure.

Tater Tot waves to MacKenzie, who checks in the guests. Then he says hello to Ms. Kris, the concierge, who knows all the fun places to go!

"Oh, Tater Tot!" cries Rose.
"Please take this menu to Chef Paul.
The birthday party begins very soon!"

Tater Tot's ears jump to the top of his
head as he replies, "Happy to help."

As Tater Tot trots toward the kitchen, Ann,
the engineer, asks, "Tater Tot, will you hold
this new light bulb while I take the broken
light bulb out?" Tater Tot is happy to help.

Sweet Ms. Janet, who lives on the thirty-fourth floor, needs help pushing the elevator button. Jim needs help tying a bow. Kuo needs help finding his pencil.

Tater Tot finally heads to the kitchen, feeling so great about helping everyone!

-MENU-
Appetizer
Soup/Salad
Entree
Dessert
Coffee

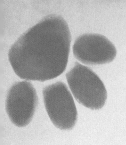

"Tater Tot, what took you so long?
We are almost out of time!" Chef Paul cries.

Tater Tot explains how he just helped everyone.

"You are very kind to help, but you said you
would bring the menu right away. We counted
on you," Chef Paul gently explains. "Now
run along. We have to rush or the birthday
guests will be mad they have no lunch!"

Tater Tot's ears slide down to his chin. He is
sorry he created this problem for Chef Paul and
the birthday guests. As Tater Tot's eyes fill with
tears, he hears the most fantastic singing.

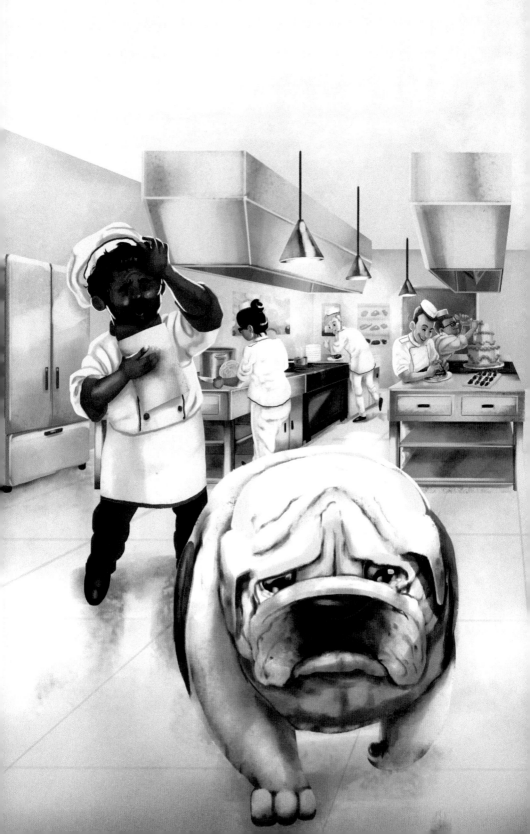

Someone's lively, booming voice
wraps around his ears like a warm hug.
Tater Tot realizes he is smiling,
even though he is still sad.

"Larry!" cries Tater Tot as he sees
the most wonderful bellman in the
world. "What are you singing?"

"My mother's favorite song!" says
Larry. "She taught me so many."

Tater Tot's ears jump from his chin to the top of
his head so fast that fur falls off each side!

"I know exactly how you can
help," Tater Tot tells Larry.

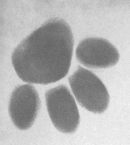

Tater Tot runs back to the kitchen,
bringing everyone he helped along the way!

"Everyone is here to help you," Tater Tot
blurts out. Chef Paul starts to ask a question,
but Tater Tot is already sprinting away,
yapping, "Don't worry, the birthday guests
will never notice their lunch is late!"

Tater Tot sees the guests already sitting and beginning to grumble about having no lunch, when suddenly the most fantastic singing comes from the back of the room.

Larry, the most wonderful bellman, sings his way through the tables, where every guest is staring in silence and smiling from ear to ear. Just as Larry finishes his last note, the guests jump out of their chairs and cheer wildly! At the same time, Chef Paul announces, "Your lunch is served!"

The guests are saying, "The Chase is the best place to have a party!"

Tater Tot snuggles in his bed, feeling proud about what he learned today. As he gently begins to snore, he imagines what he will learn tomorrow.

About the Author

Laura Holman Byrne has been Tater Tot's chief biographer since 2012. She loves seeing all the smiles and kind words Tater Tot receives from everyone he meets.

You can keep up with Tater Tot's adventures at:

www.MrTaterTot.com

 @TaterTotLessonsForLife

 @TaterTaterTot

 @TaterTaterTot

This book belongs To _____

I read this book with _____

Tater Tot's story made me think about…

Made in the USA
Coppell, TX
27 November 2019

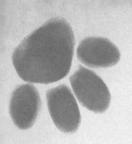

Tater Tot runs back to the kitchen,
bringing everyone he helped along the way!

"Everyone is here to help you," Tater Tot
blurts out. Chef Paul starts to ask a question,
but Tater Tot is already sprinting away,
yapping, "Don't worry, the birthday guests
will never notice their lunch is late!"

Tater Tot sees the guests already sitting
and beginning to grumble about having no
lunch, when suddenly the most fantastic
singing comes from the back of the room.

Larry, the most wonderful bellman, sings his way
through the tables, where every guest is staring
in silence and smiling from ear to ear. Just as
Larry finishes his last note, the guests jump out
of their chairs and cheer wildly! At the same time,
Chef Paul announces, "Your lunch is served!"

The guests are saying, "The Chase is
the best place to have a party!"

Tater Tot snuggles in his bed, feeling proud about what he learned today. As he gently begins to snore, he imagines what he will learn tomorrow.

About the Author

Laura Holman Byrne has been Tater Tot's chief biographer since 2012. She loves seeing all the smiles and kind words Tater Tot receives from everyone he meets.

You can keep up with Tater Tot's adventures at:

www.MrTaterTot.com

 @TaterTotLessonsForLife

 @TaterTaterTot

 @TaterTaterTot

This book belongs To _____

I read this book with _____

Tater Tot's story made me think about…

Made in the USA
Coppell, TX
27 November 2019